John Thomas McIntyre

In the Toils

John Thomas McIntyre

In the Toils

ISBN/EAN: 9783337335090

Printed in Europe, USA, Canada, Australia, Japan

Cover: Foto ©Andreas Hilbeck / pixelio.de

More available books at **www.hansebooks.com**

IN THE TOILS

A Melodrama in Five Acts

BY

John T. McIntyre

With Cast of Characters, Time in Representation, Description of
Costumes, Scene and Property Plots, Entrances and Exits,
and all of the Stage Business

Philadelphia
The Penn Publishing Company
1898

In the Toils

CAST OF CHARACTERS

NED BENINGTON . . . . *A wanderer*

ROBERT SEVEREN . . . . *A man with a fear*

GIDEON GRIND . . . . *A shyster lawyer*

JACK OAKLEIGH . . . . *An adventurer*

RICHARD MORTON . . . . *A young barrister*

BUD BRADY . . . . *A tough nut to crack*

ROB HANLON . . . . *A detective*

SLUGGER RAFFERTY . . . . *A shoulder hitter*

HELEN MORTON . . . . *Richard's sister*

MRS. BRADY . . . . *Bud's mother*

MAGGIE RILEY . . . . *Who " lives out" with Grind*

POLICEMAN, ITALIANS, STREET VENDERS, LOUNGERS, ETC.

TIME IN REPRESENTATION, ABOUT THREE HOURS.

COSTUMES

NED BENINGTON, age, about 30. Act I.—Rather loud brown check suit, somewhat worse for wear; brown derby hat; russet shoes. Has a dissipated look, and seems reckless as to consequences. Brown wig and mustache. Act II.—Same costume, but has lost his reckless look. Act III.—Well and quietly dressed. Black cutaway coat and striped trousers; black derby hat. Act IV.—Dark sack suit and derby hat. Act V.—Same as in Act IV.

GIDEON GRIND, age, about 55. Act I.—Cutaway coat and mixed trousers, both slightly shiny. Smooth shaven, gray wig. Same in Act II. Act III.—Same, with overcoat and derby hat, both a bit seedy. Act IV.—Same, without overcoat.

JACK OAKLEIGH, age, 40. Act I. Loud clothes, fairly good in quality; sack coat and silk hat. Smooth face. Same, with soft hat, in Act II. Act III.—Dark suit, derby hat, and overcoat. Act IV.—Same, without overcoat. Act V.—Same.

BUD BRADY, age, 20. Act I.—Double-breasted black or blue coat and vest; light checked trousers; tan shoes; pearl slouch hat, and red necktie. Act II.—Same. Act IV. —Same, change to black soft hat, and dark necktie. Act V.—Same as Act IV, except change to loud blue and white dotted necktie and striped trousers.

ROBERT SEVEREN, age, 50. Act III.—Elegant black cutaway coat, with dark trousers, and patent leather shoes; dark spring overcoat, and silk hat on hat tree in office. Act IV.—Same. Act. V.—Same, change to frock coat.

4

RICHARD MORTON, age, 30. Act IV.—Dark soiled clothes, light brown wig and mustache. Make up very pale. Act V.—Neat dark walking suit; dark hat, and walking stick. Has lost his pallor.

ROB HANLON, age, 30.—Act I.—Dark walking suit, with sack coat; soft hat. Change in Act II to sack suit of light material; brown derby hat. Act V.—Same as Act II.

SLUGGER RAFFERTY. Act II.—Very tough costume. Hat pulled down over eyes, and walk with elbows bent and head dropped and shoved forward.

MAGGIE RILEY, age, 18. Act I.—Loose blouse waist, rather gay in color. Sleeves rolled up in Scene 1. Short skirt; black stockings and shoes, the latter slightly run down at the heel. Hat with feathers in Scene 2. Costume should be a bit shabby. Act III.—Same, with coat. Act IV.—Newsboy costume. Tattered coat and trousers, with well-worn shoes: ragged soft hat; loose blouse shirt, open at neck. Act V.—Loose waist, dark skirt, longer than in Act I. Neat shoes and stockings. Whole costume is much neater than in previous acts.

HELEN MORTON, age, 25. Act II.—Neat walking dress of dark material; hat and coat. Act III.—Black dress and coat; linen collar and cuffs; plain black hat. Act IV.—Same.

MRS. BRADY, age, 50. Act II.—Dark colored house dress, with white kerchief crossed on bosom; red wig. Act. III.—Same, without kerchief, and with hat and coat. Act V.—Same as Act II.

Conventional dress for WAITERS, POLICEMAN, ITALIANS, etc., etc.

PROPERTIES.

ACT I.—Newspaper clipping for GRIND; detective badge for HANLON; roll of bills for OAKLEIGH; bottles, glasses, and liquors for bar.

ACT II.—Table cloth and dishes for MRS. BRADY; sewing materials, and valise with papers inside, for HELEN MORTON; revolver for RAFFERTY.

ACT III.—Duster for MRS. BRADY; revolver in desk for SEVEREN; knife for OAKLEIGH.

Act IV.—Newspapers for MAGGIE; revolvers for OAKLEIGH, BUD, and BENINGTON; knives and rope for ITALIANS.

Act V.—Call bell for SEVEREN; door bell to ring outside; two knives for SEVEREN.

SCENE PLOT

Act I

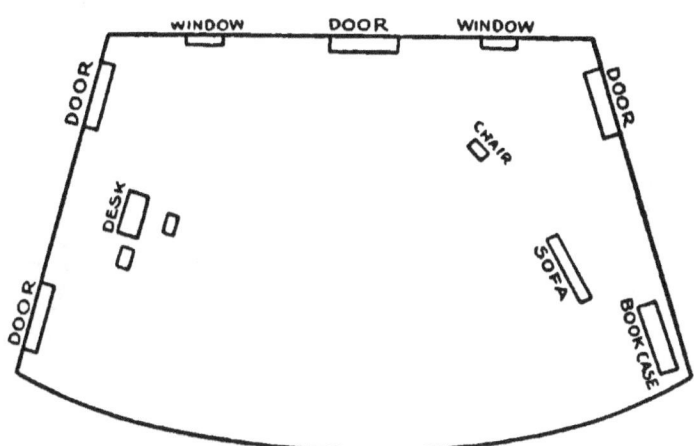

DIAGRAM OF SCENE I, ACT I

SCENE—Office setting, boxed. Rather shabby furniture. Doors, R. I E., R. U. E., L. U. E., and C. in flat. Windows R. and L. in flat. Desk and chairs R. C. Haircloth sofa and chair L. Book case with legal books down L. A motto or two on wall.

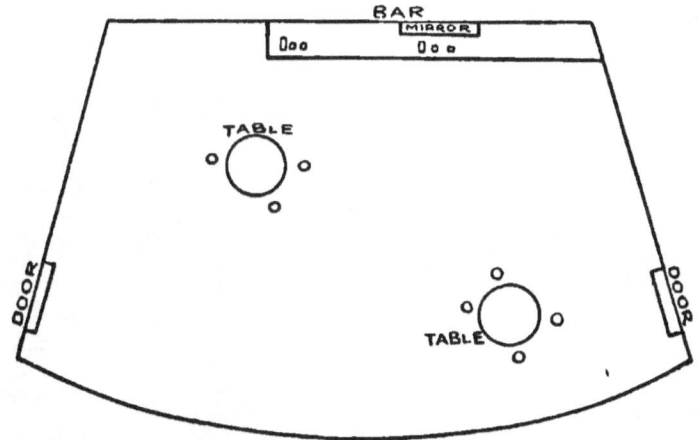

DIAGRAM OF SCENE 3, ACT I

SCENE—Café, boxed set. Doors, R. I E. and L. I E. Bar at back, with mirror, drinking glasses, and bottles. Tables up R. and down L.

Act II

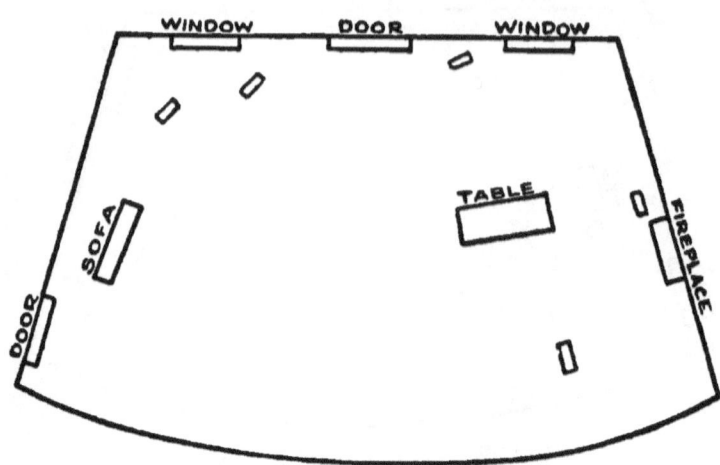

DIAGRAM OF SCENE I, ACT II

SCENE—Living room at Mrs. Brady's home. Doors
R. I E. and C. in flat.   Table L. C.   Fireplace L.   Sofa R. C.
Chairs about room.   Windows R. and L. in flat.

Act III

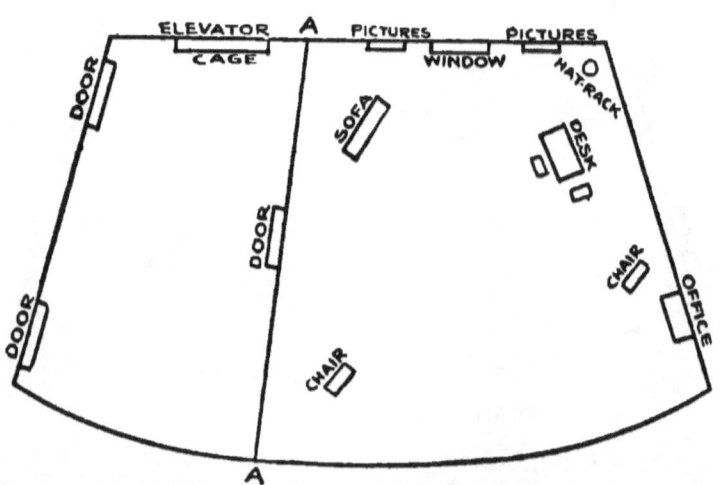

DIAGRAM OF SCENE

SCENE—Interior of Granite Office Building.   Corridor R.
Robert Severen's office, L.   Entrances R. U. E. and R. I E.
Partition A A, with practical door C.   Window L. C.   Ele-

vator cage L. in flat. Desk, with papers on top, chairs in front and at side, up L. Sofa up C. Easy chairs about room. Hat tree up L. Pictures each side of window.

ACT IV

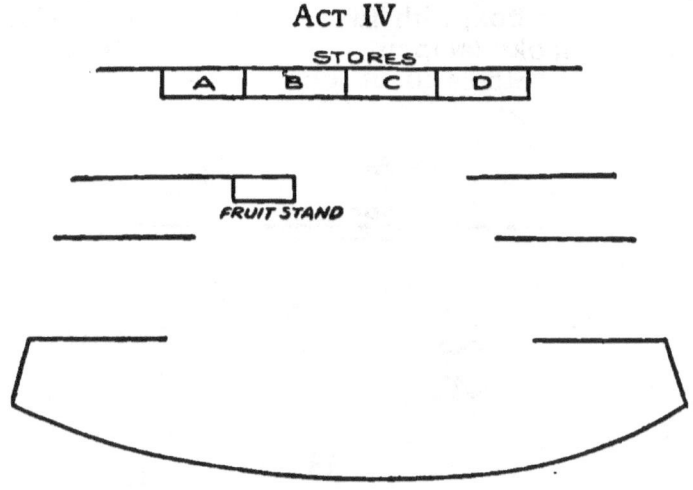

DIAGRAM OF SCENE I, ACT IV.

SCENE—A street in 4th G. Entrances R. and L. Stores in flat with wares exhibited through windows and on pavement. A, second-hand clothing store ; B, pawn shop with three gilt balls in front ; C, another clothing store ; D, butcher's shop. Italian's fruit stand on pavement up R. Pedestrians moving in front of stores. Peddlers crying their wares.

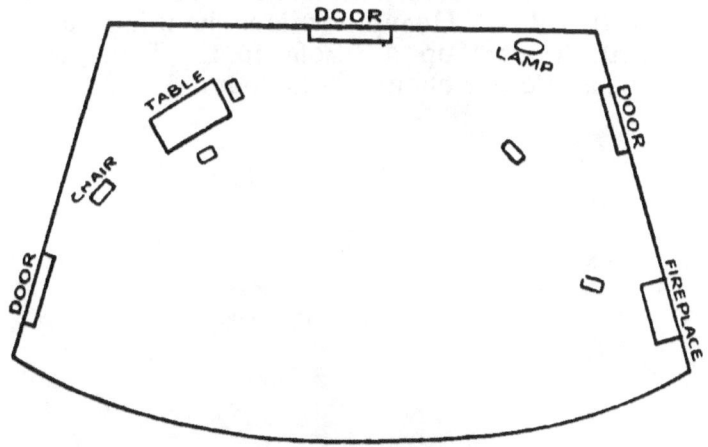

DIAGRAM OF SCENE 2, ACT IV

SCENE 2, ACT IV

SCENE—Room in tenement house, boxed set. Doors R. I E., L. U. E., and C. in flat. Rough finished walls. Table made of a large box, with two wooden stools at side and end, up R. Smoky lamp up L. Fireplace with embers of fire at L. front. Stools about room. Chair L.

ACT V

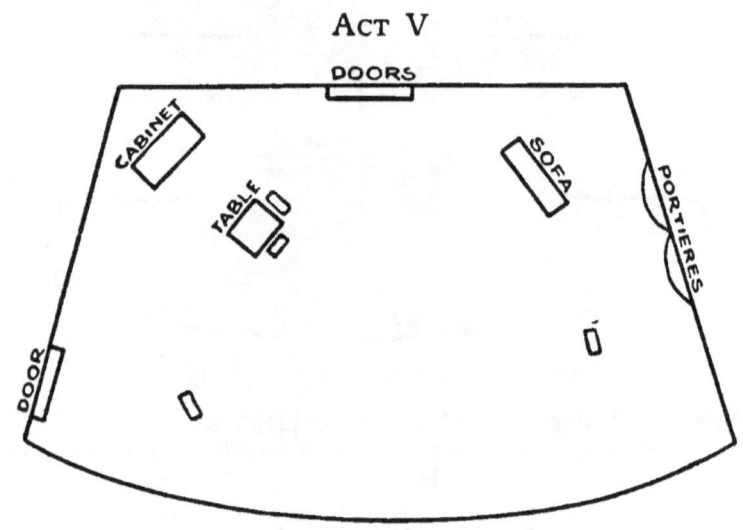

DIAGRAM OF SCENE

SCENE—Drawing room, handsomely furnished. Doors R. I E. and C. in flat. Heavy portières hanging at L. 2 E. Cabinet with drawers up R. Sofa up L. Table, with two chairs R. C., and other chairs about room.

IN THE TOILS

ACT I

SCENE 1.—*Office of* GIDEON GRIND. *For description, see scene plot. Enter* GRIND, R. 1 E.

GRIND. (*calling*) Maggie! Maggie! I say. Curse the brat, where is she now!

(*Enter* MAGGIE, L. U. E.)

MAGGIE. Were you a-callin' me?

GRIND. I have been bellowing about the house for the last half hour. Did you deliver that message to Mr. Oakleigh yesterday?

MAGGIE. Yes; I gave it right into his own hooks.

GRIND. Was there an answer?

MAGGIE. Yes, but I forgot what it was.

GRIND. Forgot! Look you, you hussy, you had better mind yourself or I'll take a whip to you.

MAGGIE. No you won't, either! You walloped me when I was a kid, but I'm too big for that now. An' you look a-here, Grindsey, I ain't no hussy, see! I'm a lady, I am, an' don't you forget it.

GRIND. Bah, you poor-house brat, you would have starved in the gutter had not I given you a home and pampered you with the best of everything. (*Sits down at desk and fumbles with papers.*)

MAGGIE. (*aside*) Best of everything! Well gee-whizz! if that's the best I wouldn't like to tackle the worst. Pickled tripe and cold water for breakfast, shadow soup for dinner and sometimes bread that you couldn't cut with a handsaw.

GRIND. Curse the man, why does he not come?

MAGGIE. (*aside*) Listen to the old sinner praying. Wonder what he'd say if he knew I read the note I took to Jack Oakleigh yesterday? I wouldn't have done it, only he forgot to seal the envelope. It's not right to put temptation in my way, like that. Grind's old enough to know better.

(*Knock at door in flat.*) Here's Oakleigh now. I'd better chase myself or the old mug 'll fire me.

(*Exit* MAGGIE, L. U. E.)

GRIND. (*Opens door*) Ah! it is he. You are late, Jack, I had given up hopes of you.

(*Enter* OAKLEIGH, *door in flat.*)

OAKLEIGH. Deuced sorry to have kept you waiting, Grind. I had urgent business that required my immediate attention. But now that I am here, what's in the wind? Something lucrative, I trust.

GRIND. Lucrative is too weak a word. If we pull the wires properly we can live like bloated bond-holders for the remainder of our lives.

OAKLEIGH. Indeed! You interest me. And now, my dear Grind, if it would not be asking too much, would you mind giving me the particulars of the little scheme you have in mind?

GRIND. Listen, and I will explain the nature of my speculation. A short time ago I happened to be out on some business and was detained until late. On my way home I stumbled over a young man who was lying on the sidewalk. At first I thought him drunk, but subsequently discovered that he was sick. He was well dressed; everything about him spoke of means. I called a cab and had him taken to my home—out of charity, of course.

OAKLEIGH. Well, that's good. I can imagine Gideon Grind picking a man out of the gutter and bringing him home out of charity. No designs upon his valuables in case he died, of course. Very good, Gideon; you are quite a humorist. (*Laughing.*)

GRIND. To cut it short, he grew delirious; from his ravings I learned that he was the representative of an English law firm, and had come to this country in search of the heir of a large estate in the south of England, one Edward Benington, formerly of Boone County, Kentucky.

OAKLEIGH. The deuce!

GRIND. I have heard you speak of an acquaintance of that name, and, if I mistake not, he hailed from that very county.

OAKLEIGH. Yes; I have a friend of that name, the last of a family regarded as being enormously wealthy in ante-bellum days. His father was a confirmed gambler, and scattered his dollars about like dirt. I met him on a Mississippi River steamer in the early sixties. The son ran away

from home at the age of sixteen, and has since been travel-
ing about the world in search of adventure. I ran across
him at a race-track a short time ago, and, as he seemed to
be pretty well heeled, I struck up an acquaintance with
him by recalling some anecdotes of his father.

GRIND. It is the very man! We are in luck, Jack.

OAKLEIGH. The deuce we are! I say, Grind, let a little
light on this matter, will you?

GRIND. This young Englishman of whom I speak has
documents, secured from the lawyer of the Boone County
Beningtons, tracing their genealogy to the time of their
emigration.

OAKLEIGH. Well?

GRIND. I know where those papers are.

OAKLEIGH. Humph! What good are they to us?

GRIND. Don't you begin to see my drift. Young Benington, according to report, has never returned to Kentucky. The friends of his boyhood would not recognize
him if they fell over him. If we secure possession of the
documents and get young Benington out of the way,
what's to hinder a young man of your talents from getting
the genealogical tree, former connections, and private trans-
actions of the Beningtons by heart, assuming the name of
Edward Benington, and laying claim to the estate?

OAKLEIGH. An excellent plan! But can it be carried
out?

GRIND. Without doubt. In the first place, you have the
confidence of young Benington. How easy it would be to
get him into a scrape and land him in jail for a good long
term.

OAKLEIGH. That's all well enough. But the young
lawyer will split when he hears of the imposition.

GRIND. I have provided for that. He is safe under lock
and key and in a place from which he would have some
difficulty in escaping.

OAKLEIGH. Good! You have a great head for detail,
Grind; pray accept my congratulations. But in regard to
the documents—you say you know where they are—the
question is, can we get them into our possession?

GRIND. I have not overlooked that point. (*Drawing
slip of paper from his pocket.*) Here is a personal which I
clipped from a newspaper. (*reads*) " Any information rela-
tive to the whereabouts of Richard Morton will be thank-
fully received by his sister, Helen Morton, 89 Blank Street."
(*To* OAKLEIGH) My barrister is the person inquired after in
the personal. From what he said during his delirium I

learned that the papers in question were in the possession of his sister, who accompanied him to this country. I have not the least doubt but that we can secure them in good time.

OAKLEIGH. Bravo, Grind! You are an arch plotter. Now it seems to me that the first step should be the cooking of Benington's goose. The trick will be easy, because the police have an eye on him on account of his shady associates. But I must leave you, Grind. I have an appointment at Maynard's with this very man. I'll see you tomorrow and we will discuss this affair in detail. Goodnight.

GRIND. Good-night, Jack; keep your eyes open.

OAKLEIGH. You can depend upon me.

(*Exit* OAKLEIGH, *door in flat.*)

GRIND. The first step is taken; I can feel half of the Benington fortune in my pocket at this moment. And it will be before many days, (*chuckling and rubbing his hands*) before many days.

(*Exit* GRIND, R. U. E., *and enter* MAGGIE, L. U. E.)

MAGGIE. Ho! Ho! Up to some more crookedness, are you, you dried up old scarecrow. Going to have a man pinched for nothin', are ye; goin' to swipe somethin' off that sick fellow's sister, are ye? Well, I guess not, Giddy, nor you either, Jack Oakleigh. I'll block your little game, or my name ain't Maggie Riley.

(*Exit* MAGGIE, *door in flat.*)

SCENE 2—*A street set in 1st* G.

(*Enter* BUD BRADY.)

BUD. Well, say, this yanks the doughnut. I'll never back another scrapper as long as I'm on the dirt. Here I goes behind the Port Richmond Cyclone, jist to oblige me friends. An' he was a peach, he was. Why, the mug that he was up against pasted the face off him. An' jist because I gave him a steer about upper-cuttin de jay, he ups an' bangs me on de mug. An' that ain't all; Reddy O'Toole jist told me that Casey, the special's, lookin' fer me wid a search warrant fer aidin' and abettin' a prize fight. It's dead wrong, that's what it is. They all impose on me because I'm little.

(Enter MAGGIE, R.)

MAGGIE. No, siree; I ain't a-goin to let that mug get pinched for nothin'—why Bud Brady!

BUD. Hello, Mag! Where ye goin' in such a rush?

MAGGIE. That's my business. You look here, Bud Brady, I've got a bone to pick with you. Where was you last night? Don't you know it was Wednesday, an' fellows always go to see their girls on Wednesday nights?

BUD. Well, look at that! Say, Mag, I forgot all about it.

MAGGIE. I don't believe it; you ain't stuck on me or you wouldn't forget to come and see me. I was onto you the other night when you were a-monkeyin' around that Katie Murphy that works for the Dublin dressmaker.

BUD. *(aside)* I knowed that 'ud get me me into trouble. *(To* MAGGIE) What I tell you is on the dead level, Mag. I was up at Casey's Hall; the Aurora Borealis Association was givin' their grand annual spasm. Say, it was out o' sight! The police backed up a patrol wagon an' pinched the whole gang. You ought to went, Mag.

MAGGIE. Indeed! Well, Mr. Brady, when I go out a-drivin' I don't do it in a patrol wagon. I am a lady, I am, even if me old man is doin' time.

BUD. I s'pose you keep a carriage now, an' pair o' grays an' a big duck with whiskers to drive 'em, eh?

MAGGIE. I never said I did. But if I was a young man an' was in love with a young lady, I'd invite her to take a spin in the park Sunday afternoons, any way.

BUD. But how could I do that? The bloke what keeps the livery stable charges two plunkers an hour for an old hat rack of a plug that you could see through. I can't afford that, Mag; I only make four per week.

MAGGIE. You always have enough to take in them scrappin' matches an' free-an'-easies, but when yer out with me yer always broke, can't even buy me a lemonade with a straw in it or a plate of pink ice-cream.

BUD. *(aside)* She's twisted because she can't pull my leg. *(To* MAGGIE) Now, say, Mag, didn't I buy you a hat full of peanuts to put in yer stockin' last Christmas? On the dead, now, didn't I?

MAGGIE. That's right! Throw it up to me! If I'd known ye'd shoot off about it afterwards I wouldn't have took 'em. *(Cries.)* Bud Brady, I'll never speak to you again as long as I live.

BUD. Ah! Say, Mag, stop yer slobberin'.

MAGGIE. *(stamping her foot)* I won't!

BUD. Ye know I'd make ye a present of a house on West

Walnut Street if I had the stuff. (*Puts his arm around her.*) Stop soakin' yer apron an' I'll take you down to Swinghammer's ice-cream joint and blow ye off to soda water.

(MAGGIE *hesitates, then lays her head on his shoulder. They exit* L., MAGGIE *still sobbing.*)

SCENE 3.—*Maynard's Café. For description, see scene plot. Bartenders and waiters about room. Enter* HANLON *and a policeman,* R. E.

HANLON. I've my eye on a pair of queer sprinklers, Slater. Make it a point to be on hand in case I need your assistance.

POLICEMAN. Very well, sir. (*Steps back to bar.*)

(*Enter* BENINGTON, L. I E., *followed by a crowd. They all walk to the bar.*)

BENINGTON. Call for what you want, boys; it's my treat. The wager was won and lost fairly.

HANLON. (*aside*) That young fellow has an honest look, but, if we are to judge men by the company they keep, he's crooked. He's been hand and glove with Jack Oakleigh, the slipperiest bird in town, for some time. I'll keep my eye on you, my friend, and find out what you're made of.

(BENINGTON *crosses over to table in centre and sits down.*)

BENINGTON. Well, this is a pretty state of affairs, I must say. Here I am, stranded in a strange city without a five in my clothes—a fitting wind-up to a roving life. For fifteen years I have wandered about the world, spending my money in dissipation. I cannot recollect one dollar that has gone to feed the hungry or clothe the naked—all went in a whirl of profitless pleasure. But now that I am at the end of my rope I will settle down. This is a good city for a man of energy; I will stay here and begin life anew. I have been an infernal fool, but my future shall radically differ from my past. To-night winds up the page of prodigality in my career; to-morrow I turn over a new leaf.

(*Enter* MAGGIE, L. I E.)

MAGGIE. (*aside*) I wonder if that man Benington's here now? Maybe this duck knows him. (*To* BENINGTON) Excuse me, mister, do you know any one by the name of Benington here?

BENINGTON. Why yes; that's my name.

MAGGIE. (*aside*) Well, look at that, I struck it the first time! (*To* BENINGTON) Well, I've got somethin' to tell ye, somethin' you'll be mighty glad to know. (*Enter* OAKLEIGH, L. I E.) Gee-whiz. (*Aside*) If there ain't that mug Oakleigh; I'd better skip or he'll drop to my game.

(*Exit* MAGGIE, R. I E.)

BENINGTON. (*looking after her.*) Well, that's a queer girl! I wonder what she wished to tell me.

OAKLEIGH. (*slapping* BENINGTON *on shoulder*) Well, Ned, my boy, how do you find things?

BENINGTON. Poor, Jack, mighty poor.

OAKLEIGH. (*laughing*) What's this, Ned Benington, the jolliest blade in the Quaker City, down with an attack of blue devils! Come, come, old man, what's the trouble, perhaps I can remedy it.

BENINGTON. In the first place I'm broke, in the second I have had an attack of conscience.

OAKLEIGH. (*laughing*) Is that all; I supposed it was something serious. Don't you know, my boy, the latter invariably follows at the heels of the former. (*Aside.*) Here's my chance: Jack Oakleigh you have the devil's own luck. (*To* BENINGTON) I happen to be pretty well heeled at present, Ned, and can loan you a hundred.

BENINGTON. Thank you, old fellow; fifty will be plenty.

OAKLEIGH. But I have nothing smaller than a hundred.

BENINGTON. Then we will break it on a bottle. (*Raps on the table and waiter crosses over.*) A bottle of dry, Jackson, and be spry!

WAITER. Yes, sir; have it here in a moment, sir. (*Goes to bar.*)

OAKLEIGH. (*handing note to* BENINGTON) Here you are, Ned; if you want any more you know where to come.

BENINGTON. Thank you, Oakleigh; I'll not forget this.

OAKLEIGH. (*aside*) No; I hardly think you will.

(*Waiter puts a bottle and glasses on table.* BENINGTON *hands him the bill.*)

WAITER. I will bring your change at once, sir.

HANLON. (*aside*) I'll have a peep at that note. (*Steps up to waiter.*) I'm a police detective. (*Shows his badge.*) Let me see that note.

WAITER. Yes, sir; here it is, sir.

OAKLEIGH. (*aside*) By all that's black, there's Hanlon, the fly cop, examining the queer. My scheme has worked quicker than I expected.   I must get out of this, or I'll go up the flue with Benington.

(*Exit* OAKLEIGH, L. 1 E.)

HANLON.   Just as I expected, counterfeit.

BENINGTON.   Hello! Where the deuce has Oakleigh gone!   Here, waiter; where's my change?

HANLON.   Ha, Oakleigh has scented danger and escaped.   I'd give five years of my life to put that man behind the bars.   But I've got his pal; that's some comfort.

BENINGTON.   Waiter, I say, hello there!   Where's my change?

HANLON.   (*laying his hand on* BENINGTON's *shoulder*) The only change you'll get, young fellow, is a change of clothes and climate.

BENINGTON.   (*rising*)   What do you mean?

HANLON.   That you are under arrest.

BENINGTON.   Under arrest!   And for what?

HANLON.   For shoving the queer.   (*To policeman*) Slater, take this man in charge.

(*Policeman seizes* BENINGTON.)

BENINGTON.   Release me, you scoundrel, or you shall repent this outrage upon an innocent man.

HANLON.   I would advise you to keep quiet, young fellow; everything you say now will be used against you at the trial.

(*Enter* BUD *and* MAGGIE, R. 1 E.)

BENINGTON.   Trial!   Do you mean to say that I shall be compelled to submit to the indignity of a trial for an offense I unwittingly committed.   I declare before Heaven that I am guiltless of intentional crime!

BUD.   That's on the dead level, Mr. Hanlon.   That man's innocent, an' what's more, he's the victim of a plot.

HANLON.
WAITERS.
POLICEMAN.   } The victim of a plot?
LOUNGERS.

MAGGIE.   Yes, the victim of a plot, an' I can prove it!

CURTAIN

ACT II

SCENE 1.—MRS. BRADY'S *home. For description, see scene plot.* MRS. BRADY *arranging the tea table.* HELEN *sewing.*

MRS. BRADY. Shure, I dunno what could have come over him at all, at all. Five weeks is a murderin' long time to shtay away widout sayin' a word. An' then to leave his sister all alone in a strange place, wid divil a cent till bless herself wid. Faix it beats me, so it do, an' that's the truth.

HELEN. He complained of feeling unwell when I last saw him, and I have often thought that, perhaps, he had been taken ill among strangers who, not knowing him, have been unable to communicate with me.

MRS. BRADY. But, shure, you went to the police station an' all av the hospitals, an' sorra the thing could they tell ye about yer missin' brother.

HELEN. (*weeping*) No, nothing, Mrs. Brady. I sometimes think him dead.

MRS. BRADY. Tut, tut, tut! Sorra the bit av him's dead. You'll soon have him back alive an' well. (*Aside*) It wouldn't do to tell her, but I've been to the morgue ivery mornin' fur a week back, an' ivery time expectin' to see him stretched out cold an' stiff. He had money about him an' he's met wid foul play, an' that's the opinion of Nancy Brady.

HELEN. Another thing of which I wished to speak is your disinterested kindness. But for you I should now be friendless, penniless and homeless in this great city. Poor Richard had all our funds and letter of credit upon his person when he disappeared, and upon his failure to return—

MRS. BRADY. The blaguard landlord turned you out. Divil a stroke av work I've done fer him since, the thafe av the world!

HELEN. I should have gone mad in my despair had you not held out a helping hand, given me a home and found me employment. I can never thank you sufficiently for your kindness to a poor, friendless girl.

MRS. BRADY. Arrah! darlin', don't be talkin' to me. I only wish I could give ye a better home than this an' feed ye on spring chicken instead of kidney stew. Shure here I'm blatherin' here (*blustering about*), an' Bud'll soon be home, an' will be as mad as a hatter if his supper ain't standin' ready fer him. Musha! but I don't know what's

19

come over the boy since he took up wid the gang of blaguards on the corner beyant. He's gettin' to be a regular scalawag, so he is. To see the walk on him (*swaggering about*) you'd think he owned the biggest part av the City Hall. (*Enter* BUD, *door in flat.*) Ah! here's the blaguard now.

BUD. How do, Miss Morton? Heard anything of your brother yet?

HELEN. No, Bud, nothing; and I sadly fear I never shall.

BUD. Don't say that! Ye've always got a chance until yer laid out stiff. Your brother's all hunkey. I'll bet he's out on a batter, and'll turn up all O. K. when he gets braced up. Supper ready, mom?

MRS. BRADY. Faith an' it's not, an' it won't be for an hour.

BUD. Well, say! Yer dead slow! Get a move on, will ye? I'm goin' down to O'Hallihan's to see a scrap.

MRS. BRADY. Begorra, them scrappin' matches'll be the death av ye yet; d'ye mind that, now?

BUD. Ah! Yer twisted, old lady. I can put up my fives with any of 'em, see! (*Strikes pugilistic attitude and dances about.*)

MRS. BRADY. Arrah, look at the style of the spalpeen, look at him now! (*Seizing a plate from the table.*) Sit down, ye omadhaun, or I'll knock ye down.

BUD. What do ye think of me style, mom?

MRS. BRADY. Faith, an' I'll knock some of the style out av ye if ye don't keep better hours. Where were ye last night?

BUD. Oh, down to Maynard's Café.

MRS. BRADY. Maynard's Café, is it? An' what the divil were ye doin' in a swell place like that?

BUD. Why, ye see, the beaks pinched a bloke an' took him to the jug in a ding-ding.

MRS. BRADY. The beaks pinched a bloke, is it? Faith, an' Mrs. Flannigan's parrot pinched me wid his beak last Monday, an' begorra, I kin feel it yet. But what the divil's a bloke an' a ding-ding, I dunno. Bud Brady, I want ye to keep away from that Slim Jim's laundry! Sure I believe the pig-tailed blaguard's been learnin' ye to jabber Chinese!

BUD. Oh, ye don't catch on. A beak's a copper an' a bloke's a man. The man was arrested for shovin' the queer.

MRS. BRADY. Oh, that's it! Why the divil didn't ye say

that in the first place, an' not go blatherin' about ding-dings an' the like av that? Did ye know the man?

BUD. His name was Edward Benington. He said he came from Kentucky.

HELEN. Edward Benington! And from Kentucky! Why, that is the name and native place of the man Richard was in search of. The name is a most uncommon one. Surely this is not a coincidence.

MRS. BRADY. Arrah, look at that, now. Here he has a fortune comin' to him an' gets himself into jail for passin' counterfeit money. It'll be a long time a-fore he'll enjoy his good luck, I'm thinkin'.

(*A knock at door in flat.*)

BUD. That's some one knockin' at the door, mom.

MRS. BRADY. Av course there is you lu-nat-ic! D'ye think the door could knock at itself? Open it an' see who's there.

BUD. (*opening door*) Well, what d'ye want?

(*Enter* SLUGGER RAFFERTY, C.)

SLUGGER. I'm lookin' fer a young lady named Morton.

HELEN. (*arising*) That is my name.

SLUGGER. I've got a note fer ye from a duck that says he's yer brother. (*Hands her the note.*)

HELEN. My brother! Thank God! Tidings from him at last! Now a weight is lifted from my heart in the knowledge that he is alive. Where is he? (*To* SLUGGER) Why did he not communicate with me before and relieve me of this dreadful suspense?

SLUGGER. Don't know. Maybe the note'll tell ye.

(HELEN *opens envelope and reads.*)

BUD. (*aside to* MRS. BRADY.) Say mom; d'ye know who that tough-lookin' mug is?

MRS. BRADY. I do not, an' I don't want to. D'ye think I have nothin' to do but go around gettin' acquainted wid tough mugs, as ye call thim?

BUD. That's Slugger Rafferty, the collar-an'-elbow wrestler. He can down anything in the ward from a glass of lager to Duckey McFee.

MRS. BRADY. From the looks av him, I think he practices most on the lager.

HELEN. Richard has been ill, is not yet strong enough to leave his bed. Oh, Mrs. Brady; to think of his tossing in the agonies of fever and me not beside him to nurse him back to health and life. He asks me to come to him at once (*putting on her bonnet and coat*), and desires me to bring the papers concerning the Benington case with me.

MRS. B'RADY. But you'll wait for supper, Miss Helen. Do, darlin'; it'll give ye strength.

HELEN. No; I must go at once. I cannot delay an instant. The documents are in my grip; I shall take them as Richard directs.

(*Exit* HELEN, R. I E.)

SLUGGER. Say, old woman, tell her to get a gait on, will ye?

MRS. BRADY. Old woman, is it? Begorra, ye black muzzled divil, I want ye to know that I'm no old woman; d'ye mind that now?

SLUGGER. Ah, don't git cranky about it; I don't want no muss with a woman, I don't, see?

BUD. Well, say, ye galvanized Turk, maybe ye'd like a little mix up with the old woman's son? Take off yer coat an' I'll thump yer ribs loose. (*Squaring off at* SLUGGER.)

SLUGGER. Ah, what's the matter with ye, ye chump! I'd paralyze ye in a punch.

MRS. BRADY. Here, here! I'll have no monkey shines in this house. Shut up now or I'll settle the pair av ye.

(*Enter* HELEN, R. I E., *with small valise.*)

HELEN. I am quite ready. Good-bye, dear Mrs. Brady (*kissing her*); you were my only friend in the hour of need. Good-bye, Bud.

BUD. Good-bye, Miss Morton,

(*Exit* HELEN *and* SLUGGER, C.)

MRS. BRADY. (*calling from doorway*) Good-bye, darlin'! Don't forget to let us know how yer poor brother s gettin' on. (*Closing the door*) Arrah, but she's the sweet creature!

BUD. Ain't she, though. Say, I wish she'd do that to me. (*Smacking his lips.*)

MRS. BRADY. Do what?

BUD. Kiss me; yum! yum!

MRS. BRADY. Kiss ye, is it? Begorra, ye Port Richmond dude, d'ye think a real lady like that would kiss a big, dirty-faced blackguard like ye?

BUD. Why, ain't I good looking?

MRS. BRADY. Arrah, go long out av that! (*Seizing a broom*) If ye don't want yer looks spoiled, ye'll quit makin' a show av yerself.

BUD. But on the dead level, I don't like this.

MRS. BRADY. An' ye'll like it less if I welt ye wid this broom.

BUD. Ah! I ain't kiddin' now. I mean I don't like Miss Morton's goin' out with that duck, Rafferty. He's a tough nut, he is; he'd strangle his grandmother for the price of the growler.

MRS. BRADY. Shure, Buddy boy, when I come to think av it, the spalpeen had a divilish look. Whorra! Whorra! Why did I let her go at all, at all!

BUD. I'll chase 'em up, an' if Rafferty tries to ring in any crooked work, down goes his shanty.

(*Exit* BUD, C.)

MRS. BRADY. (*calling from doorway*) Bud Brady, if ye don't bring Miss Helen back safe an' sound, an' smash the divil out of that schooner-hoister Rafferty, I'll have ye sent to the penitentiary for life. (*Closing door*) Somethin' bad'll happen to the creature. I feel it in me bones. Whorra! Whorra! Why did I let her go! An' Bud, too. I hope he won't get hurt. Begorra! the young blaguard would fly at the divil himself if his blood were up.

(*Exit* MRS. BRADY, R. I E.)

SCENE 2.—*Exterior of* GRIND'S *office, set in 1st G. Door in flat, C., leading into office. Entrances R. and L. Lights half up. Enter* HELEN *and* SLUGGER RAFFERTY, R.

SLUGGER. This is the house. (*Knocks at the door in flat.*)

HELEN. (*aside*) I am getting nervous. The neighborhood is so deserted and the buildings so dark and gloomy.

(*Door opens and enter* GRIND, C.)

SLUGGER. This is the lady you sent me for.

GRIND. Ah, my dear young lady! I'm delighted at your coming. The young man can hardly restrain his impatience to see you. (*Aside*) And that's the truth, only the young man happens to be Jack Oakleigh.

HELEN. Oh, sir, take me to him at once! I have been so long in suspense that I cannot delay seeing him one moment longer than is necessary.

GRIND. You are not a whit more anxious than he is. Will you walk in?

SLUGGER. (*aside*) To my parlor, said the spider to the fly.

(*They all exit, door in flat. Enter* BUD, R.)

BUD. Well, I'm onto the joint he's steered her to. It was the old duck that Mag works for that let 'em in. I could see that front of his five blocks away. Well, say (*looking up at house*), Miss Morton's brother might be in that ranch, but I don't believe it. Anything old Grind puts his hooks on must pan out the gilt, an' he ain't particular what it is. I think I'll put me lamps on the back part of this shebang ; maybe I can get inside an' find out what's on the carpet.

(*Exit* BUD, L., *and enter* BENINGTON, R.)

BENINGTON. Well, this is a most surprising train of events. That girl, Maggie Riley, is a brick. She not only succeeded in getting me out of the clutches of the law but showed me that Jack Oakleigh, a man whom I deemed my best friend, gave me the bogus money for the sole purpose of getting me into trouble. Well and good, Mr. Oakleigh ! I will endeavor to return the compliment, and perhaps in an equally disagreeable manner.

(*Enter* HANLON, L.)

HANLON. Ah! Well met, Mr. Benington ; accept my apologies for the trouble I gave you last night. Will you shake hands? I trust you bear me no ill will.

BENINGTON. Certainly not. Appearances were against me, and you but did what you thought your duty (*shake hands*).

HANLON. You show your good sense. There is something in store for you. This girl, Maggie Riley, has put me on the track of an exceedingly sharp game. I cannot reveal its nature at present, but subsequent developments will prove most surprising to you. By the way, I want to give you a tip. When you get into a strange city, don't grow intimate with every gentlemanly fellow you run across. Men of Oakleigh's stamp have ruined more young men than any other sort of crook in the city.

BENINGTON. Thank you ; your advice is good.

HANLON. I must leave you, as I have work on hand that will keep me jumping till morning. Good-night.

BENINGTON. Good-night.

(*Exit* HANLON, R., *and enter* BUD, L.)

BUD. (*aside*) I'm dead sure now that there's something crooked goin' on. I heard that fly duck Oakleigh chinnin' to old Grind, an' when that team pulls together straight people want to keep their lamps wide open. Hello!—blame me, if there ain't the young fellow that Oakleigh tried to put in the jug. Now if I go a-huntin' up the cops I might be too late to help Miss Morton. I'll bet a nickel this fellow's dead sore on Oakleigh an' 'ud go into this thing with me if I gave him the brace. Excuse me, young fellow (*to* BEN-INGTON), I want to ask you a question.

BENINGTON. A dozen if you wish.

BUD. One'll do the trick. Don't a gentleman always help a lady in distress?

BENINGTON. A true gentleman will do so, always.

BUD. On the dead, now, are you a gentleman?

BENINGTON. Well-er-yes; I make some pretension to the title.

BUD. A pair of crooked mugs has steered a lady into that joint there. I ain't onto their game, but you can bet yer life it's on the cross. You know one of the birds; his name is Oakleigh.

BENINGTON. Oakleigh, well he's a greater scoundrel than I imagined. My friend, if I can be of any assistance to the lady I am at your service. It shall never be said that Ned Benington refused succor to a woman in distress.

BUD. Say, when I first put me lamps on you I knowed you were built on the correct plan, There's a window open around at the back of the house. An' say, when we once get inside, an' I get a chance to put up me hooks with that mug Rafferty, I'll put him to sleep so quick that he'll think he was struck by lightnin'.

(*Exit* BUD *and* BENINGTON, L.)

SCENE 3. *Interior of* GRIND'S *office, same as Act 1, Scene 1. For description, see scene plot. Enter* GRIND *and* HELEN, *door in flat.*

HELEN. I beg of you, sir, to take me to my brother immediately.

GRIND. Restrain yourself, my dear young lady; you shall see him in good time. Meanwhile I desire to ask a few questions.

HELEN. Proceed, sir.

GRIND. First, allow me to summon a very dear friend of Richard's, a very dear friend indeed. Mr. Oakleigh (*calling*),

(*Enter* OAKLEIGH, *left door.*)

Allow me to present, Miss Morton, your brother's firmest friend. Oakleigh, this is Richard's sister.

(HELEN *and* OAKLEIGH *bow.*)

OAKLEIGH. Miss Morton, I am delighted. (*Aside*) Fine girl, that.

GRIND. With your permission, Miss Morton, we will now proceed to business. Your brother's mission to America was to hunt up the heir of a certain estate, was it not?

HELEN. It was, sir.

GRIND. He has important documents, proving the rightful claim of one Edward Benington, of Boone County, Kentucky, has he not?

HELEN. You have been correctly informed, sir. (*Aside*) I begin to fear these men. What means all this questioning?

GRIND. In the note written at your brother's dictation, he requested you to bring these documents with you. Have you done so?

OAKLEIGH. (*aside*) The point at last!

HELEN. I have done as Richard desired.

OAKLEIGH. (*aside*) Good!

GRIND. (*rubbing his hands*) Will you let me see them?

HELEN. The documents are of great importance. I shall require to see my brother first, then act according to his desires.

OAKLEIGH. (*aside*) Humph! It will be more difficult than we anticipated.

GRIND. But, my dear young lady, your brother has authorized me to examine them.

HELEN. You will pardon me if I insist upon seeing him before the papers leave my possession.

GRIND. And I insist that you turn them over to me. Jack, lock the door!

(OAKLEIGH *locks door in flat.*)

HELEN. What is the meaning of this?

OAKLEIGH. It means that we want those papers and intend to have them.

GRIND. And that we have a nice little cage to lock you up in until Jack Oakleigh proves to the satisfaction of the trustees of the estate that he is Edward Benington.

HELEN. Oh, Heaven! I see it all now. You have decoyed me here to rob me of the papers entrusted to my care! But you shall not have them; I will defend my trust with my life!

OAKLEIGH. You had better submit, girl.

HELEN. You shall kill me first. Allow me to go from this place at once and unmolested, or I shall give an alarm. (OAKLEIGH *seizes her, and* GRIND *takes the documents from the grip*) Help! Help!

OAKLEIGH. Hush! you little fool; there is no one here to help you!

(*Enter* BENINGTON, R. I E.)

BENINGTON. You mistake, Jack Oakleigh; I am here!

OAKLEIGH. (*releasing* HELEN) The deuce! (*Grasping* GRIND'S *arm*.) It's Edward Benington.

HELEN. Oh, sir! Save me from these ruffians I implore of you!

GRIND. (*to* OAKLEIGH) The foul fiend, seize him; how came he here?

BENINGTON. Compose yourself, Miss; you are perfectly safe under my protection.

OAKLEIGH. You are out there, Ned Benington; you have played directly into our hands. Instead of one prisoner we now have two (*calling*). Rafferty! (*Enter* SLUGGER, *left door*.) Cover that man! (SLUGGER *draws revolver and points it at* BENINGTON.) If he attempts to move, shoot him down! Now, Ned Benington, who holds the winning hand? (*Enter* BUD *through window in flat, seizes revolver and knocks down* SLUGGER.)

BUD. (*pointing revolver at* OAKLEIGH *and* GRIND) Bud Brady, you brace of beats; an' it's a full house!

QUICK CURTAIN

ACT III

SCENE.—*Corridor in the Granite Office Building.* SEV-
EREN'S *office,* L. *For description, see scene plot.* SEV-
EREN *seated at desk reading letter.*

SEVEREN. So this very perplexing hunt is ended at last,
and the heir of the Benington millions has made his appearance. Well, I am heartily glad of it; the case has been a
most complicated one. Let me see; the heir writes that
he will call at noon. I trust he will have no difficulty in
proving his identity, as I should like to wind up the affair
at once and have done with it.

(*Enter* MRS. BRADY *and* MAGGIE., R. I E.)

MAGGIE. Say, them elevators is out o' sight. This beats
keepin' house for old Grind all to bits, Mrs. Brady. Since
you got me here helpin' you to clean these offices I'm hav-
in' a dead easy thing of it. A steam lift to hoist me up to
the tenth floor, an' a'most nothin' to do when I get there.

MRS. BRADY. Arrah, quit yer clatter, Maggie allanna!
or we wont get started to-day. This is Mr. Severen's day,
an' if there's any one inside we'll have to roust them out.
(*Knocks at office door.*)

SEVEREN. Come in.

MRS. BRADY. (*entering office with* MAGGIE) Good-mornin'
to ye, Mr. Severen. It's sorry I am to be disturbin' ye, sir;
this is yer cleanin' day, an' we've come to slick up a bit.

SEVEREN. True, Mrs. Brady; I had forgotten (*rising
and taking up his hat and overcoat from hat tree*). I will
attend to some outside business and be out of your way at
the same time.

(*Exit* SEVEREN, *closing office door*, R. I E.)

MRS. BRADY. (*removing hat and coat*) Arrah! but he's
the nice man. A real gentleman, if there ever was wan.

MAGGIE. Say, Mrs. Brady, you know Bud?

MRS. BRADY. Of course I know Bud! Shure, an' it 'ud
be a queer thing if I didn't know me own son.

MAGGIE. Well–er–did he tell ye that—I mean did he
tell ye anything?

MRS. BRADY. Faith an' he did, that! He told me that he
swept the sidewalk with Owen Grady's boy Dinnis fer
callin' me a red-headed owld scarecrow, more power to
him.

28

MAGGIE. Didn't he tell ye anything else?

MRS. BRADY. Divil a thing. (*Bustling about with duster and arranging things on desk.*)

MAGGIE. Didn't he tell ye that me an' him was engaged?

MRS. BRADY. Engaged, is it! Faith he did not, or I'd a-broke the blaguard's head!

MAGGIE. Well, it's true; we are engaged.

MRS. BRADY. Shure yer jokin'.

MAGGIE. Not a bit; you can ask Bud himself.

MRS. BRADY. Is it you that's engaged to my boy, Bud?

MAGGIE. To your boy, Bud.

MRS. BRADY. (*laughing*) Arrah, begorra that takes the cake! Bud Brady engaged, an' him only makin' four dollars a week! (*Laughing*) Shure the big gommouch must be crazy and ye must be the same, Maggie Riley. Troth, the pair av ye could starve to death right nicely on that much money!

MAGGIE. But we're not going to be married till Bud gets his job in the post-office. He says he's got a pull in his division, an' it won't be long.

MRS. BRADY. But, sure, if ye are not goin' to be married, what the divil are ye engaged for, I dunno?

MAGGIE. Because (*sobbing*) I love Bud and Bud loves me. (*Cries.*)

MRS. BRADY. (*aside*) Shure an' I do believe that she thinks well of the boy. Arrah, don't cry, darlin'. (*To* MAGGIE) I was only jokin'.

(*Enter* BENINGTON *and* HELEN, R. U. E.)

I'd rather have yerself fer my Bud's wife than any other girl in the world. (*They embrace.*)

HELEN. Are you quite sure that Mr. Severen's office is on this floor?

BENINGTON. The porter said so, at any rate. Ah! here it is. (*Knocks at office door.*)

MRS. BRADY. Hush, Maggie, allanna; there's some one at the door. (*Opens door*) Shure, an' is it yourself, Miss Helen, and ye, too, Mr. Benington!

HELEN. What! You here, you dear, good old soul! (*Kisses* MRS. BRADY.)

BENINGTON. Good morning, Mrs. Brady. We have called to see Mr. Severen.

MRS. BRADY. An' he's jis this minute gone out. I suppose it's advice ye'd be after askin' of him. Troth an' if they came to me for advice (*aside*), I'd tell them to go to the first parson, faith an' I would that.

MAGGIE. Say, Mr. Benington, I seen old Grind and Jack Oakleigh this mornin'; why don't ye have them pinched fer kidnappin' Miss Morton?

BENINGTON. Simply because Mr. Hanlon advised me not to do so. He is of the opinion that if given plenty of rope they will, eventually, hang themselves. Do you think Mr. Severen will be gone long, Mrs. Brady?

MRS. BRADY. He didn't say, sir; but it's meself that's expectin' him back directly.

BENINGTON. Then we will wait.

MRS. BRADY. Very well, sir. (*Aside*) Come, Maggie, don't ye see we're in the way? Shure an' if two's a company an' three's a crowd, begorra four's a whole mob (*going*).

HELEN. I trust we have not interfered with your duties, Mrs. Brady.

MRS. BRADY. Not a bit av it, not a bit.

(*Exit* MRS. BRADY *and* MAGGIE, R. I E.)

BENINGTON. What a veritable rough diamond is that woman! So crude and primitive without, but perfect and flawless within.

HELEN. I alone know the full measure of her kindness.

BENINGTON. (*Aside*) Now is my golden opportunity. Brace up, Ned; there's no telling when you shall again have a chance so favorable.

HELEN. A penny for your thoughts, Mr. Benington.

BENINGTON. I was thinking of one of God's fairest creatures.

HELEN. Which one of them, pray?

BENINGTON. A woman.

HELEN. Indeed! (*Turning away*.)

BENINGTON. Need I say who that woman is? (*Taking her hand*.) Need I say that it is yourself?

HELEN. Mr. Benington!

BENINGTON. Nay, do not seek to withdraw your hand; let me keep it in my possession forever. I love you, Helen; love you with all the ardor and strength of my soul. My love for you is the purest and holiest thing in my life. It is not a sudden attachment that springs up one moment only to die the next; but one that has had time to mature and ripen; the love of a man who, though young in years, is old in experience. When I first saw you I had the good fortune to save you from injury in a runaway accident. You were then but a girl, yet your face has remained graven on my heart. For months I hunted the streets of London in the hope of meeting you again, but in vain. I knew not where to seek ; I was ignorant of even your name. But I meet you again, after the lapse of five long years, and again have the happiness of saving you from danger—a danger incurred in a brave defense of my rights. Lest you again slip out of my life, I make bold to tell you of my love, and ask you to become my wife. Miss Morton—Helen—say that one little word, a word that will make me the happiest fellow in all this world.

HELEN. Since the time of which you speak the image of my gallant preserver has been enshrined within my heart. Since that time a love for him has been smoldering within my breast. And now it bursts into flame and compels me to answer—Yes.

BENINGTON. My darling ! (*They embrace.*) My cup of joy is full ! Soon, when I have balked the designs of those schemers, you shall be the charming mistress of my home, and I the proud possessor of the sweetest little wife in all the world.

HELEN. Don't flatter me ; you will find me like other girls. We all have our faults.

BENINGTON. True, but yours must be charming ones. At any rate, I am willing to take you as you stand, the bad qualities along with the good. But come. Mr. Severen seems determined not to return as long as we remain. Let us take a stroll ; by the time we return he shall, perhaps, have put in his appearance.

HELEN. Willingly ; the air is very close and oppressive. (*They go out into the corridor.*)

BENINGTON. I believe that the police headquarters is somewhere in this neighborhood. We will call there and endeavor to see Mr. Hanlon, and learn what progress he is making toward the recovery of my family records.

(*Exit* BENINGTON *and* HELEN, R. U. E.)

(*Enter* SEVEREN, R. I E.)

SEVEREN. (*entering office*).Humph ! My caller has not yet arrived. (*Sitting down at desk and taking up papers.*) Rather dilatory, it seems to me.

(*Enter* OAKLEIGH, R. I E.)

OAKLEIGH. Now for some delicate manœuvering. It

will require the touch of a master to play the part up to the standard of a shrewd lawyer. (*Knocks at office door.*)

SEVEREN.   Come in.

OAKLEIGH. (*entering office*) Have I the honor of addressing Mr. Severen?

SEVEREN.   I am Mr. Severen.   Be seated, sir; to what am I indebted for the honor of this—(*Staggering back.*)   Merciful Heaven!   Jack Oakleigh!

OAKLEIGH. (*aside*) My old pal, Bob Severen, by all that's black!   Curse the luck, why was I not warned by the name. I must persuade him that he is mistaken or all is lost. (*To SEVEREN*) Sir, I perceive that you have mistaken me for another.

SEVEREN.   Mistaken!   Would to Heaven that I were. You are that infamous blackleg, Jack Oakleigh.   I have good cause to remember you.   I paid you a price for your silence and to leave the country.   I demand to know why you have returned,

OAKLEIGH. (*aside*) This is the devil's own mess. Ah; by the eternal, I have an idea.   My power over him now is as great as it was ten years ago.   (*To SEVEREN*) I will admit that I was once known as Jack Oakleigh, but my true name is Edward Benington.

SEVEREN.   What!   You Edward Benington!

OAKLEIGH.   I am Edward Benington, and have documents proving my rightful claim to the Benington estate.

SEVEREN.   Ha!   So that is your game?   You may depend that I shall nip it in the bud.

OAKLEIGH.   You will not.

SEVEREN.   I know you to be an impostor and will denounce you as such.

OAKLEIGH.   Again I say you will not.   Denounce me as an impostor and I will denounce you as a murderer.

SEVEREN.   Hush!   For pity's sake, hush!   Some one may hear!

OAKLEIGH. (*laughing*) Ah, that brings you to your senses does it?   You probably forgot why you paid me the sum of five thousand dollars some ten years ago.   Bob Severen, the law has not forgotten your crime.   I can send you to the gibbet at my pleasure.   Listen to me: With your assistance I can prove to the satisfaction of the trustees of the estate that I am the heir.   Refuse to aid me, and you suffer the consequences.

SEVEREN.   Man, have you no pity in your heart?   Have mercy upon my family if you will have none upon me.

OAKLEIGH.   It rests solely in your own hands. Co-operate with me, or I will brand you as an assassin!

SEVEREN. You must give me time—I cannot think—my brain is in a whirl! Merciful Heaven! I shall go mad. (*Sinks down at his desk.*)

OAKLEIGH. (*looking at his watch*) I can give you but a short time to consider. My lawyer waits below. I shall return with him in a few moments and shall expect a definite answer. (*Going, and pausing at the door*) Remember what awaits you should you refuse. (*Goes into the corridor*) The game is ours; all is over but the shouting.

(*Exit* OAKLEIGH, R. I E.)

SEVEREN. This is terrible. My one great sin recoils upon me! To have him reappear after all these years of seeming security makes it doubly hard to bear. He is destitute of conscience, and would crush me like a worm were I to refuse his demands. There is but one mode of escape (*opens drawer in desk and takes out revolver*), and that is here. It requires but a slight pressure of the finger and care and trouble will be things of the past. But, were I to commit self-murder, what would it avail me? 'Tis not for myself I fear, but for the disgrace the revelation would bring upon my wife and boy. That man is a fiend incarnate; he would pursue me even beyond the grave, and by blacking my memory, would visit upon the head of my innocent boy the ignominy of his father's crime. No! no! 'tis a cowardly and needless act; I would sink my soul into perdition and it would avail me naught.

(*Enter* GRIND *and* OAKLEIGH, R. I E.)

OAKLEIGH. As my lawyer, Grind, you will inform Severen that you intend taking immediate steps to secure possession of the estate in my behalf. If he admits in your presence that I am Edward Benington, all is well; and should young Benington turn up we shall feel safe. (*Knocks at door and enters office, followed by* GRIND.)

SEVEREN. (*arising*) What, so soon!

OAKLEIGH. Just so. I desire to present my attorney, Mr. Grind. (*Aside to* SEVEREN) Not a word in his presence.

GRIND. (*bowing*) I am delighted to meet so eminent a gentleman. I have taken the liberty of waiting upon you, sir, in behalf of my client, Mr. Benington.

SEVEREN. You must pardon me; I can give no information regarding the case until I have had time to weigh the proofs of your client's identity. I must have more time to enter into this affair; (*aside to* OAKLEIGH) otherwise you can do your worst.

OAKLEIGH. (*aside*) I must not goad him too far. (*To* SEVEREN) Very well, we will call in a day or two. Mr. Grind will leave the documents proving my identity. Perhaps when we call again you will be ready to talk business.

(*He opens office door and steps out into corridor, followed by* GRIND. SEVEREN *stands in doorway. Enter* BENINGTON *and* HELEN, R. 1 E.)

BENINGTON. (*to* HELEN) And now, having seen Mr. Hanlon— What! Grind and Oakleigh here!

GRIND. (*to* SEVEREN) My client, sir, possesses all the necessary documents and can prove to the satisfaction of the English courts that he is Edward Benington.

BENINGTON. (*advancing*) You lie! you shriveled old scoundrel!

OAKLEIGH. Curse the luck! That fellow again!

BENINGTON. (*to* SEVEREN) You are Mr. Severen, I presume. Sir, I am Edward Benington; that man (*pointing to* OAKLEIGH) is an impostor!

OAKLEIGH. You lie, curse you!

GRIND. (*aside to* OAKLEIGH) Now is the time to test your power over Severen. Bring him to his knees now or you never will.

OAKLEIGH. (*aside to* SEVEREN) The time has come to declare in my favor. Refuse, and by Heaven I will hand you over to the law.

SEVEREN. (*Aside to* OAKLEIGH) Spare me! In Heaven's name, do not compel me to commit this crime!

OAKLEIGH. (*still aside*) You have the alternative— choose!

SEVEREN. (*to* BENINGTON) Sir, I am convinced that this man is the person I seek!

BENINGTON. Then you, too, are leagued with these rascals to defraud me of my rights! Is this the way you guard your trust?

SEVEREN. (*aside*) This is more than I can endure! I shall go mad! mad! (*Enters office and sinks down at desk.*)

BENINGTON. Then I am to understand that I have three to cope with. Well, the more the merrier. I shall find means to thwart you all. Take heed, you precious pair of scoundrels! They say the devil takes care of his own; if this be true, he will require the thousand eyes of Argus and need to keep his vigil incessantly to guard you from my vengeance. (*Walks up the stage.*)

OAKLEIGH. (*aside to* GRIND) We shall have trouble with

that young fool. I recommend silencing him at once, for good and all. Are you with me, Grind?

GRIND. To the death!

OAKLEIGH. Good! We must get the girl out of the way also. (*Takes off his coat and hands it to* GRIND) Throw this over her head to prevent any outcry. Then carry her down to our hack and drive, as though the devil were after you, to Nicola's; I'll attend to the rest.

(GRIND *throws coat over* HELEN'S *head.*)

HELEN. Help! help!

BENINGTON. (*rushing upon* GRIND) Unhand her, you infernal scoundrel!

(OAKLEIGH *seizes* BENINGTON, *but is thrown off.* BENINGTON *turns upon him.*)

OAKLEIGH. (*drawing knife*) You have crossed my path for the last time.

(BENINGTON *closes with him and is stabbed.*)

BENINGTON. Good Heaven! I am stabbed! (*Falls to the floor.*)

(*Exit* GRIND, *carrying* HELEN, R. I E.)

SEVEREN. (*springing up*) What's that? It sounded like a struggle. (*Opens door.*)

BENINGTON. Helen! Helen! Where are you? They have abducted her! Jack Oakleigh, your coward's life shall pay for this day's work! (*Endeavors to rise.*)

OAKLEIGH. Curse you, I'll make a clean job of it!

(*He rushes at* BENINGTON *with the knife, but* SEVEREN *confronts him with drawn revolver.*)

SEVEREN. Back, you murderous wretch! Lay but a hand upon him and I will rid the world of one viper, at least.

QUICK CURTAIN

ACT IV

SCENE I.—*South Street on Saturday night. Night lights.*
For description, see scene plot. A crowd passing to and
fro. Venders crying out their wares. Enter OAKLEIGH
and GRIND, L.

OAKLEIGH. Well, well! I did not credit you with so
much enthusiasm in the cause, Grind. What a blood-
thirsty old reprobate you are, to be sure. But you are
wrong; the less bloodshed we have the better for all hands
concerned—especially the victims.

GRIND. Bah! You are growing chicken-hearted.

OAKLEIGH. No; only sensible.

GRIND. We can't keep them prisoners forever. We
must, in the long run, either liberate them—or kill them.

OAKLEIGH. The former mode is preferable to the latter.

GRIND. And the moment they secure their liberty they
will denounce us.

OAKLEIGH. That does not necessarily follow. I have a
way to prevent it.

GRIND. Indeed! And how would you proceed?

OAKLEIGH. I shall marry the girl.

GRIND. Marry her! You are jesting.

OAKLEIGH. I was never more serious in my life. The
fact is, the witch has captivated me. She is a lovely girl,
full of fire and spirit, just the sort of a woman I admire.

GRIND. Ah! I see; you are in love. But look you, Jack
Oakleigh, if you imperil our prospects by your nonsense I
will be revenged.

OAKLEIGH. How dense you can be, Grind, when you
have the mind. Can you not see that I intend marrying
her as much through self-interest as for her charms.

GRIND. Explain yourself.

OAKLEIGH. As can be easily perceived, the girl is proud
of both her birth and social standing. Were I once her
husband she would not proclaim me an impostor, of course
not for my sake, but for her own. It is hardly likely that
she would allow any qualms of conscience to mar her social
position. I have had much to do with women and know
the animal well.

GRIND. But her brother?

OAKLEIGH. She would prevail upon him to act likewise
and for a like reason.

36

GRIND. All easy enough—to talk about. You have overlooked the most important point—will the girl consent?

OAKLEIGH. Of course not.

GRIND. And how do you propose to surmount that obstacle?

OAKLEIGH. We will use threats.

GRIND. As we have discovered, she is not a girl to be intimidated by threats.

OAKLEIGH. Perhaps not—but we have her brother in our power.

GRIND. Ha! You mean—

OAKLEIGH. To force her to comply through fear of injury to her brother.

(*Enter* MAGGIE, *disguised as a newsboy*, L. E.)

GRIND. Good! It strikes me that your plan is a feasible one.

MAGGIE. (*calling out*) Here's your Bulletin an' Telegraph. Telegraph, sir? (*To* GRIND.)

GRIND. No! Get out!

MAGGIE. Full account of the sluggin' match in Smoky Hollow.

GRIND. Be off with you, or I'll call an officer!

MAGGIE. Baboon escaped from the Zoo; from the description he must be your brother. Don't yer want ter hear from yer long-lost relation?

GRIND. If I get my hands on you— (*Makes a rush at* MAGGIE.)

MAGGIE. (*eluding him*) Say, ye old mug, if ye hit me, I'll put the gang onto ye, an' they'll punch that front of yours, see?

OAKLEIGH. Come, come, Grind. (*Laughing*) Don't bother with the gutter-snipe. He's too many for you. (*They walk* R.) It will require us to put my plan into immediate execution; delay may ruin all.

(*Exit* GRIND *and* OAKLEIGH, R.)

MAGGIE. (*calling after them*) Go throw mud at yerself, ye old mummy; go up to the City Hall and look for yerself in the rogues' gallery. Just come back here again an' I'll paste ye in the teeth. That's the flyest pair of crooks outside of Cherry Hill. (*Soliloquizing*) But I'll find out where they've got Miss Morton if I have to dog 'em for a month. I ain't doin' a thing but cuttin' a caper in these duds of Jimmy O'Brien's. Frocks ain't in the same game. Hello!

There they go around the corner. Here ye are! Paper!
Full account of the butchery in Lombard Street!

(*Exit* MAGGIE, R.   *Enter* BUD *and* BENINGTON, L.)

BENINGTON.   This is the place where Maggie agreed to
meet us and report progress, is it not?

BUD.   Correct.   D'ye see that big window in the Dutch
bakery over there?

BENINGTON.   That one yonder?

BUD.   That's the one. I broke that with an organ-grinder
the other night.   An' would you believe it, the Dutchman
got twisted an' wanted to have me pinched.

BENINGTON.   (*laughing*) Very rude in him, I'm sure.
We are early (*looking at watch*); it lacks a half-hour of the
appointed time.

BUD.   It's only by good luck yer here at all.   If Jack
Oakleigh had put his knife into the right spot yer friends
would have been invited to meet at two and go at three.

BENINGTON.   Not good luck, Bud, but the will of Provi-
dence.   Had not my watch-case turned the blade, it would,
in all probability, have finished me.   As it was, it inflicted
a wound that momentarily deprived me of my strength.
Doubtless that rascal, Oakleigh, believes me dead.

BUD.   He tried to make sure of it, that's a fact.

BENINGTON.   I have Robert Severen to thank for my pres-
ervation.   What an impenetrable man is that! After openly
declaring himself leagued with my foes he saves my life,
when to have left me perish would have furthered their in-
terests.   His motives are inexplicable; I cannot fathom
them.

BUD.   It'll all come hunkey, after a while.   Hello! here
comes Maggie.   Say, she makes a birdy boy, don't she?

(*Enter* MAGGIE, R.)

MAGGIE.   We've got 'em! I've cornered 'em at last.

BENINGTON. }
BUD.   } Where?

MAGGIE.   On Carpenter Street, in the big Italian tenement! Miss Morton's there as sure as Mickey Flaraty's
cross-eyed.

BUD.   That's a tough joint! Them dagoes would stick a
bloke with a stiletto as quick as they would push the
pitcher.

BENINGTON.   If it were the lower regions, I'd enter it in
quest of her.   Come, we will secure the assistance of the
police.

BUD. Hold on! (*grasping his arm.*) Don't be in a rush. Get the police an' ye'll make a mess of it. If the dagoes saw a squad of coppers comin' they'd slope an' we'd lose our game.

BENINGTON. Then, in Heaven's name! what's to be done?

BUD. What's the matter with doin' the job ourselves? You've got a gun an' so have I. Let us once get inside that shebang an' we'll make things hum!

BENINGTON. Then let us go at once. Good Heavens! We know not what is happening her—and I idling here. (*Starts toward* R.)

BUD. Don't get rattled. Just go rushin' into things head first an' the gutter snipes will cook yer goose.

BENINGTON. You are right. It will require a cool head and a steady hand to outwit these scoundrels. Maggie, follow after us and watch on the outside after we enter the house. If we do not reappear within an hour, summon the police.

MAGGIE. I'll have a patrol wagon down there in two shakes.

BENINGTON. And now for desperate work. Come, Bud, and summon all your grit.

BUD. I'm good for any three dagoes in the city. If they kick up a muss, I'll fill Carpenter Street full of busted macaroni.

(*All exit*, R.)

SCENE 2.—*The interior of an Italian tenement house. Lights down. For description, see scene plot. Enter* HELEN, R.

HELEN. What a fateful journey this has been! Little did I dream when I left my London home that such an experience awaited me in America. Imprisoned in this vile den by men, who in their cupidity would not hesitate at actual murder. Hesitate! they have already committed it! Did I not hear Ned cry out that he was stabbed? Did I not hear him fall to the floor in, possibly, his death agonies? And Richard! what have they done with him? If they have crimsoned their hands in the life blood of one man, would they hesitate at the repetition of the crime? Good Heavens, these men are demons! Why should I undergo all this? What have I done to merit all this suffering? I cannot endure it; I would that I were dead! Then, at least, I should be free from the clutches of these monsters.

(*Exit* HELEN, L., *and enter* BENINGTON *and* BUD, *door in flat.*)

BENINGTON.   Thus far we have succeeded in evading detection.   But I fear to open a door lest some of these Italian thugs be behind it.

BUD.   We must lay low an' wait.   Ha! there's some one coming.   We are in for it now.

BENINGTON.   Never say die. If their intentions be hostile, we will give them a warm reception.

BUD.   Pull yer gun!   (*They draw revolvers.*)

(*Enter two Italians, door in flat.*)

FIRST ITALIAN.   Diavolo!   Who are you?

SECOND ITALIAN.   What-a for you-a com-a here?

BENINGTON.   (*to* BUD) We must take them off their guard if possible.   (*To Italians*) We are health inspectors and have come to look into the sanitary arrangements of this house.

FIRST ITALIAN.   You-a lie!   You-a com-a here to-a spy!

SECOND ITALIAN.   You-a never leave-a this house alive! (*They both draw knives.*)

BENINGTON.   Hold!   (*Pointing revolver*) Another step and you are dead men.

BUD.   Drop them pig-stickers (*points revolver*), or I'll put a slug in yer thinkers.

(*The Italians drop their knives.*)

BENINGTON.   Bud, open that door.

(BUD *opens door*, R.)

Now, you pretty pair, face about and march into that room.

(*The Italians hesitate.*)

BUD.   March, you son of an organ grinder, march!

(*They all exit* R.   *Enter* HELEN, L.)

HELEN.   I fancied I heard voices!   Ah!   They are returning.   I will not withdraw, but confront them and demand my liberty.

(*Enter* GRIND *and* OAKLEIGH, *door in flat.*)

GRIND.   Ah!   Here is the fair enslaver, Jack.   You have an excellent eye for female beauty.

OAKLEIGH. I trust I see you in good health, Miss Morton.

HELEN. Health never intrudes itself upon such a squalid den as this.

OAKLEIGH. You need not remain here, if you so desire.

HELEN. Have I ever expressed a desire to remain?

OAKLEIGH. You do not grasp the meaning.

HELEN. Then do not speak in enigmas, sir.

OAKLEIGH. I have the honor of making you a proposal.

HELEN. Of what nature, sir?

OAKLEIGH. Of marriage.

HELEN. Sir, you insult me!

OAKLEIGH. My proposal is a perfectly honorable one.

HELEN. Honorable! What has a man such as you in common with honor?

GRIND. Have a care, girl! We are not to be trifled with.

HELEN. I care not for your threats. Though but a weak, defenseless girl, I defy and despise you!

OAKLEIGH. Would you prefer remaining a prisoner in this filthy place to being happy as my wife?

HELEN. I would pass the remainder of my life in abject misery rather than become the wife of a man whose hands are stained with human blood!

OAKLEIGH. I see that threats of a personal nature will not affright you. But we shall see how you stand the test which I have prepared. Grind, bring him in.

(*Exit* GRIND, *door in flat.*)

Helen Morton, I have determined that you shall be my wife, by fair means or foul. I have already exercised the fair; now I shall try the foul.

(*Enter* GRIND, MORTON, BUD, *and* BENINGTON, *door in flat, the two latter disguised as Italians.* MORTON'S *hands are bound behind his back.*)

MORTON. Helen! How came you here?

HELEN. Richard! My brother! (*Rushes toward him.*) `

OAKLEIGH. (*grasping her arm*) That will follow in good time.

GRIND. (*to* MORTON) We have brought her here to comfort you, my dear sir; to comfort and console you. (*Chuckling.*)

MORTON. You treacherous toad! (*Kicks him.*) I often

wonder why Heaven permitted such a viper as you to pass from under its creating hand and live!

OAKLEIGH. Enough of this. We are not here to pay doubtful compliments, but for business. Richard Morton, I have just made your sister a proposal of marriage, and she has refused.

MORTON. Refused! (*Struggling with* BENINGTON *and* BUD, *who hold him*) Curse you! If I were free I would strangle you!

OAKLEIGH. Compose yourself and listen to reason. I asked your sister's hand as a gentleman should.

MORTON. A gentleman!

OAKLEIGH. She refused me. We now mean to adopt measures to force her to comply.

HELEN. Threats will not avail you. Though you torture me, I will still refuse!

OAKLEIGH. We shall see. (*To supposed Italians*) Do your work. (*They stir up embers in fireplace, and put several small iron bars into the flames.*) We shall now try a new mode of persuasion.

HELEN. Merciful Heaven! What would you do?

OAKLEIGH. In their own country these men were brigands, and were accustomed to torturing their prisoners until they forced them to pay a ransom for their release. Do you see those irons? They will soon be at a white heat. Swear to become my wife within four-and-twenty hours, or your brother shall be turned over to the tender mercies of these men!

HELEN. Demon! You dare not!

OAKLEIGH. You shall see. Bind him to that chair (*to supposed Italians*).

(*They bind* MORTON *to the chair.*)

GRIND. When you hear the hiss of his burning flesh you will be glad to accede to our demands.

MORTON. She shall never consent, you fiends; though you murder me, she shall still refuse!

HELEN. Are you human? Has your greed for gold frozen every stream of kindness in your hearts! Do what you will with me, but spare my brother (*falls upon her knees*). See, upon my knees I implore you not to commit this dreadful deed.

OAKLEIGH. Do you consent?

MORTON. She shall never consent.

GRIND. Do your work, men.

HELEN.   No, no, no; in God's name I appeal to you (*to supposed Italians*).

OAKLEIGH.   Curse you, you yellow-skinned dogs! Will you do as you are bid?

BENINGTON.   We will not.

GRIND.   That is not Nicola's voice! (*Grasping* OAK-LEIGH'S *arm*.)   These men are spies!

OAKLEIGH.   Spies! Then they shall never live to tell of what they saw here this night.   (*Draws revolver.*)

BUD.   Another step and I'll make a sieve out of ye. (*Points revolver.*)

GRIND.   Who are you, in the fiend's name?

(BENINGTON *and* BUD *throw off their disguises.*)

BENINGTON.   Friends of the helpless and champions of persecuted!

QUICK CURTAIN

ACT V

SCENE.—*Drawing-room in house of* ROBERT SEVEREN. *For description see scene plot.* SEVEREN *seated at a table*, R.

SEVEREN. This villainous piece of business has gone too far. The insolent effrontery of that scoundrel, Oakleigh, has roused within me a spirit of desperation and defiance. I will submit to his dictation no longer—driven to bay even the rat will turn and show its fangs. He has hounded me with the relentless persistency of a blood-hound, rendering me capable of any deed to throw off his intolerable yoke. He shall swear this night to haunt me no more, or his hand shall lose its cunning and his lips be sealed forever in the darkness of the grave. (*Rings bell.*)

(*Enter* MAGGIE, *door in flat.*)

MAGGIE. Did you ring, sir?
SEVEREN. I did. I am expecting a visitor. When he arrives show him here. Do you understand?
MAGGIE. Yes, sir.
SEVEREN. My sole reason for engaging you and Mrs. Brady during the absence of my family and servants, was that I could depend upon you not to pry into what did not concern you. Under no circumstances must yourself or Mrs. Brady molest me during my interview with the person I am expecting.
MAGGIE. Very well, sir.

(*Exit* MAGGIE, *door in flat.*)

SEVEREN. Should this meeting terminate as I fear it will, I am prepared to engage these conspirators with their own weapons, black treachery, low cunning, and—if occasion demands—violence.

(*Exit* SEVEREN, R. 1 E., *and enter* BUD, *door in flat.*)

BUD. Well, say! (*looking around*) This goes right up front. The old woman and Mag will be too swell to talk to a fellow if they hang up their hats in this joint long. But they won't be long here if they don't keep their lamps open. The front door was wide open an' I waltzed right in without sendin' up me card. They want to put a chain on that openin' or some fly duck'll float in here an' swipe the silver. I wonder where Mag an' the old woman is?

44

(*Enter* MAGGIE, *door in flat.*)

MAGGIE. Gee-whiz! If there ain't Bud. Well, don't he just look on the front seat of the band-wagon. But I'm something of a swell now meself. Just watch me knock him off his balance. (*Coughs.*)

BUD. (*perceiving her*) Hello, Mag! I was just wonderin' what part of the joint ye hung up in. Say, ye look right up to date in them new duds.

MAGGIE. Sir! How dare you address me without an introduction? How dare you call my habiliments duds?

BUD. Eh!

MAGGIE. Have you suddenly become bereft of the sense of hearing, or are your educational deficiencies the cause of your failure to comprehend what I articulate. (*Aside*) That ought to stupefy him.

BUD. The grub ain't good in this neighborhood, Mag, is it? Been lunchin' off Webster's Unabridged, eh?

MAGGIE. The feed's out o' sight. But, oh, Bud, when I walk around this scrumptious drawing-room I must sling a big bluff or I'd bust. Say, Bud! How nice you look in yer new polka-dot tie. An' say; on the dead now (*feeling the leg of his trousers*) how much did you give fer the bags?

BUD. A dollar thirteen. The dollar was plugged an' I got Goldenstein to chalk up the thirteen till pay-day. But I've got slashin' good news, Mag; a job in the post-office, salary one hundred a month, an' it's a lead-pipe cinch; all I've got to do is to fire the bums off the steps. We can come up to the scratch now, Mag; say the word, an' we'll get the knot tied a-Sunday.

MAGGIE. Oh, Bud! Won't that be nice. (*Embracing him.*)

BUD. Well, ye can just bet your sweet life it will. But that ain't all. Ye know that little brick house at the end of McGerrigal's Alley? Well, McGerrigal says he'll let us have it fer three plunkers a month cheaper than any one else, because I licked the tax-collector fer him one day last week.

MAGGIE. Won't that be just on the top of the heap!

BUD. Won't it though! But I've got somethin' else yet. When I was buyin' the togs I struck a bargain with Goldenstein. He's goin' to furnish the joint fer us—an' he's goin' to do it cheap. If he don't I'll take the gang down there an' we'll clean out the shebang.

MAGGIE. An' just to think; when we are housekeepin' I can dust, an' sweep, an' cook, an' make the bed, an' have

everything lookin' nice when you come home from work.
An' in the evenin' you can smoke yer pipe—

BUD.   An' push the can if any of our friends come to see
us.   I tell ye, Mag, it'll be bang up!

MAGGIE.   I'll be awful glad to have a home of my own.
I ain't had one since mother died an' the old man started
to booze.   (*Cries.*)

BUD.   An' ye were only a kid then, too.   I remember
when ye lived in Slattery's Court an' chased the bottle fer
the old man.   Ye've had hard lines, Mag, but it's all over
now.   Ye'll never be sorry for it if ye run double with me.
I'm a tough mug, but me heart's all right.   Shut off the
water-works, Mag; after we're married I'll give ye me
wages every Saturday night.   (MAGGIE *embraces him.*)

(*Enter* MRS. BRADY, *door in flat.*)

MRS. BRADY.   (*aside*) Arrah, would ye look at them slobberin' over one another!   What the divil's Maggie a-cryin'
about, I dunno?

BUD.   But say, Mag.   There's one thing I don't like.

MAGGIE.   What's that?

BUD.   I don't like to leave the old woman.

MRS. BRADY.   (*aside*) Lave me, is it!   Begorra, they're
goin' to be married!

MAGGIE.   Leave her!   Why, say, Bud, ain't she goin' to
hang up her bonnet with us?

BUD.   I'd like her to, but—

MAGGIE.   You thought I'd kick, eh?

BUD.   That's just it.

MAGGIE.   I thought you were acquainted with me!   Your
mother's a real old Irish lady.   She was a mother to me
after me own mother died.   D'ye think, after that, I'd take
her son away from her an' give her the go-by?   You look
here, Bud Brady; if she don't put her feet under our table,
I'll give ye the dead shake, an' marry Hans Swartz, the
Dutch butcher.

MRS. BRADY.   Oh!   That's the darlin'!   She wouldn't
see a poor old creature left alone.   (*Weeps loudly.*)

BUD.   Sufferin' Jerusalem!   There's the old woman, an'
she's piped off all we said!

MRS. BRADY.   (*holding out her arms*) Maggie, darlin'.

MAGGIE.   Mrs. Brady!

(*They embrace and weep together.*)

MRS. BRADY.   Oh, the blaguard!   To want to leave his
poor old mother all alone!

BUD. But say, mom! I didn't want to leave ye.

MAGGIE. Yes, you did; you said you did. (*Still weeping.*)

BUD. Well, say, this is enough to drive a fellow to smoke cigarettes.

(*A bell rings off* L. C.)

MAGGIE. (*drying her eyes*) It's the man Mr. Severen's been expectin'. I'm to show him in here.

(*Exit* MAGGIE, *door in flat.*)

MRS. BRADY. Come down to the kitchen, me bucko (*takes* BUD *by the ear*). Leave your old mother, will ye, ye thafe av the world. Faith an' I'll knock that out av yer head, if I break a flat-iron doin' it.

(*They exit,* R. I E., MRS. BRADY *leading* BUD *by the ear. Enter* MAGGIE *and* BENINGTON, *door in flat.*)

MAGGIE. Mr. Severen's been expectin' ye. Sit down; he'll be here in a minute.

(*Exit* MAGGIE, *door in flat.*)

BENINGTON. Expecting me! There must be some mistake, Maggie— Hello, she's gone. Can it be that Severen has anticipated this visit and prepared some plausible— pshaw! I am harsh with the man. Calm reflection makes it obvious that he was forced to act as he has. I shall endeavor to wring a confession from him. (*A bell rings off* L. C.) Ah! It seems that Severen is to have another caller.

(*Enter* MAGGIE, *door in flat.*)

MAGGIE. Mr. Benington, it's Jack Oakleigh. I left the front door open an' he's comin' down the hall.

BENINGTON. Ah! Coming to have a conference with Severen, I'll be bound. Could I but overhear what will be said— Ha! the portières—the very thing! Not a word (*to* MAGGIE) to Severen or Oakleigh that I am here.

MAGGIE. Quick! Here he is. (BENINGTON *conceals himself behind the portières.*)

(*Enter* OAKLEIGH, *door in flat.*)

OAKLEIGH. The door was ajar and I took the liberty of walking in. Pray announce me to Mr. Severen. (*Exit* MAGGIE, *door in flat.*) This would be a neat crib for a good professional to try his hand on. I shall have to give the boys a tip.

(*Enter* SEVEREN, *door in flat.*)

SEVEREN. Ah! You have arrived. (*Looking at his watch*) You are punctual.

OAKLEIGH. And now that I'm here, what do you want?

SEVEREN. To talk over this imposition, this scheme to defraud young Benington of his rights.

OAKLEIGH. I thought this matter settled for good. You acknowledged me the rightful claimant in the presence of Benington himself, and have since written the English authorities that everything is settled.

SEVEREN. I have communicated no such intelligence, and, what is more, do not intend doing so.

OAKLEIGH. Bob Severen, if I thought you were playing me false, I would—

SEVEREN. No threats. I have done with you and your schemes. I refuse to be a party to your villainy. Furthermore, you shall forego this nefarious plot and keep your lips sealed concerning any act of mine of which you may have knowledge.

OAKLEIGH. (*laughing*) You don't ask much, Severen; in fact, you are quite modest. (*Grasping his arm*) You forget that I hold your reputation, your very life, in the hollow of my hand. And yet you presume to dictate to me as to what I shall and shall not do. You forget, my good friend, what an interesting story I could tell the police officials of New York City. You forget that the body of a man was found one morning, shot through the heart, in a deserted gambling hell. The murderer was never discovered, and the fact has been a thorn in the side of the authorities ever since. I need hardly say that they would be delighted if informed where they could lay their hands upon him. And this information I propose to give them if you do not act strictly in accordance with my desire.

SEVEREN. You scoundrel! You know full well that I shot John Ogden in self-defense.

BENINGTON. (*aside*) John Ogden! Can it be the same! If so, I begin to see the light.

OAKLEIGH. Perhaps so. But would a jury believe me, the witness, or you, the accused murderer?

SEVEREN. Stop! No more insults, or you shall rue it. John Ogden, as you know, drew his weapon on me because I accused him of cheating at cards. My act was clearly one of self-preservation. You were the only witness to the affair, and, like the contemptible scoundrel that you are, you threatened to denounce me as a murderer unless I paid a heavy sum for your silence. In my terror I allowed you to bleed me, to spare my family the disgrace of a trial. But do you think because I was weak enough to allow you to extort money from me then that I will submit to you exerting your power over me whenever it pleases you to do so? No, Jack Oakleigh, you have a different man to deal with. Do you remember the concluding words of my note requesting your presence here to-night?

OAKLEIGH. I can't say that I do.

SEVEREN. Then I will refresh your memory. The words were these: " Call at the hour named, and we will settle this matter once and forever." I have endeavored to persuade you to forego your purpose, but in vain. There remains but one other mode of argument. (*Opens a drawer in the cabinet.*)

OAKLEIGH. (*aside*) The fool must have taken leave of his senses to defy me in this way!

(SEVEREN *takes two knives from the drawer and throws them upon the floor.*)

SEVEREN. Select the one which you prefer.

OAKLEIGH. Severen! What would you do?

SEVEREN. Give you a chance for your cowardly life. You have hunted me down, and now I stand at bay. Take up one of those knives and fight for your life.

OAKLEIGH. And if I refuse?

SEVEREN. Then I will kill you with as little compunction as I would a rabid dog.

OAKLEIGH. (*aside*) This is more than I bargained for. The man is stark, staring mad.

SEVEREN. Quick! I will give you ten seconds to choose. (*Walks toward the portières.*)

OAKLEIGH. (*aside*) You would murder me, would you? (*Picks up one of the knives, holds it behind him and advances toward* SEVEREN.) I do not desire any violence, Severen; (*to* SEVEREN) doubtless we can come to a peaceable understanding.

SEVEREN. It must be one thing or the other. I will not parley or—

OAKLEIGH. Then die, you fool! (*Striking at him with knife.*)

BENINGTON. (*dashing the knife from his hand*) Not just yet, my friend!

SEVEREN. } Benington!
OAKLEIGH. } Curse you, you again!

BENINGTON. Your humble servant.

SEVEREN. You have saved my life!

BENINGTON. Then we are quits. (OAKLEIGH *makes for door in flat, but* BENINGTON *bars his way.*) You are not leaving us so soon, my boy. Stay a little, I have a story to tell which will interest you and Mr. Severen exceedingly. Mr. Severen, doubtless you are surprised at my presence in your house. I came with the intention of thanking you for saving me from the murderous ferocity of this gentleman (*bowing to* OAKLEIGH), little dreaming that I should have the opportunity of clearing myself of the debt of gratitude I owed you. During your conference I overheard Oakleigh accuse you of the murder of a certain John Ogden. You will be greatly surprised to learn that I have proof positive that John Ogden is still alive.

SEVEREN. Merciful Heaven, I thank thee!

OAKLEIGH. It's an infernal lie!

BENINGTON. It is the truth. You could not have seen the newspaper accounts, Mr. Severen, of the finding of Ogden desperately wounded, and of his refusal to give the name of his assailant.

SEVEREN. No. I left the city at once in order to leave my crime as far behind as possible. I forbore reading the newspapers that I might forget.

BENINGTON. That accounts for it. Perhaps you are surprised at my intimate knowledge of the case. The fact is, I met this same John Ogden at Monte Carlo about a year ago. We became very intimate and, in a communicative moment, he told me of his narrow escape from death.

SEVEREN. Then this man's power over me is at an end. I now see my way clear toward securing you your rights and placing him behind prison bars.

OAKLEIGH. (*aside*) It seems to me the jig's up, (*Aloud*) Surely you would not be so cruel. (*To* SEVEREN) What! Put a former crony behind the bars of a nasty jail! Perish the thought. You are not yourself, you are excited, confused, and will think better of it anon.

SEVEREN. Your flippancy will not save you.

(*A bell rings off* L. C.)

Hark! There is some one at the door. (*Taps bell on table.*)

(*Enter* MAGGIE, *door in flat.*)

See who is at the door.

(*Exit* MAGGIE, *door in flat.*)

OAKLEIGH. Don't you know, my dear fellow, that Scripture admonishes those who would be virtuous to turn the other cheek to those who have smitten them upon one side. If you act in strict accordance with this beautiful precept you will refrain from giving me into custody and allow me to play out my hand.

(*Enter* MAGGIE, *door in flat.*)

MAGGIE. It's old Grindsey, an' he's pinched!

(*Enter, door in flat,* HANLON, GRIND, *and* POLICEMAN. POLICEMAN *holding* GRIND *by the shoulder.*)

BENINGTON. Ho! Ho! It seems that our other conspirator is also in the toils.

OAKLEIGH. Ah! They have apprehended my esteemed co-laborer. (*Aside*) I must get out of this. (*Edges toward the door in flat.*)

HANLON. I trust you will pardon this intrusion, Mr. Severen. My man, who was shadowing Oakleigh, informed me that he entered this house. I have taken the liberty of entering in quest of him.

(*A bell rings off* L. C.)

SEVEREN. Maggie, attend.

(*Exit* MAGGIE, *door in flat.*)

There's no apology necessary, Mr. Hanlon; your prisoner is here.

(OAKLEIGH *makes a dash for the door in flat. Enter* BUD *and confronts him.*)

BUD. No ye don't. We're not done with ye yet, Oakey, old man.

(*Enter* MAGGIE, MORTON, *and* HELEN, *door in flat.*)

MAGGIE. Mr. an' Miss Morton.

MORTON. Pardon me, Mr. Severen, I did not know that you were engaged. What! Oakleigh and Grind in custody. Then I am relieved of the task of being a law unto myself.

SEVEREN. Yes; they are in a fair way of receiving their just dues at last, and the Benington estate has found an heir.

MORTON. Then my business in America is ended. I shall return to England as soon as possible.

BENINGTON. You shall return alone. Your sister remains in the land of the free and the home of the brave. She has consented to become Mrs. Benington at once.

HELEN. You are not angry, Richard?

MORTON. Angry! Why should I be? You would be married some time or other, and I may as well lose you now as later. Another thing (*extending his hand to* BENINGTON) your affianced is a man after my own heart.

BENINGTON. (*shaking his hand*) You shall never repent giving her to me. It shall ever be my foremost thought to make her happy.

HANLON. With your permission, Mr. Severen, we will remove the prisoners.

OAKLEIGH. Well, good-bye, everybody. I trust that you will call upon us now and then, even if it is only to make inquiries concerning our health.

GRIND. My curse, my black bitter curse, rest upon you all.

POLICEMAN. Here, here! None of that. Strike a gait now, or I'll club you.

(*Enter* MRS. BRADY, *right door*.)

MRS. BRADY. Ah, ha! So yer pinched at last, are ye, ye old son av a gun? Bad luck go with you to yer big boarding house on Cherry Hill!

(*Exit* HANLON, GRIND, OAKLEIGH, *and* POLICEMAN, *door in flat*.)

BENINGTON. Here are friends to whom we owe not a little. (*Shakes hands with* BUD *and* MAGGIE.) You shall never regret having raised your hands in defense of the helpless.

BUD. I always did have a hankerin' for the under dog in a fight.

MAGGIE. I'd a-done almost anything to knock the pins from under the feet of that leather-faced shrimp, Grind.

BUD. Ladies and gents, me an Mag's goin' to be spliced next Sunday afternoon, an' we invite you all to the weddin.'

MRS. BRADY. An' if ye'll come it's a good time ye'll have. Troth an' I'll make my Bud's weddin' take the shine off any that's ever took place in the ward.

HELEN. Dear Mrs. Brady, I want to thank you for all your goodness to me, and my brother also wishes to thank you. (MORTON *shakes* MRS. BRADY'S *hand*.) We can never repay you—never.

MRS. BRADY. Then don't try, darlin'. So this is yer

brother. Faith, it's many a time I gave him up fer dead, I did that.

MORTON. But you see I am very much alive. We can afford to look back upon it all and treat it as an unpleasant dream.

SEVEREN. To me it shall ever be a dreadful reality. For days I have felt that my name, my very life, hung in the balance. But, thank Heaven, I am forever OUT OF THE TOILS.

SLOW CURTAIN

www.ingramcontent.com/pod-product-compliance
Lightning Source LLC
Chambersburg PA
CBHW021232260626
47172CB00002B/722